Fabulous Franko

and his Fabulous Toys

Written by
Jane Matlock

&

Illustrated by
Kate Seeley

2nd Edition

Published in United States of America
Under license by Think-a-lot Toys Inc 2010
www.fabulousfranko.com

Design by Kate Seeley

Printed and bound in the United State of America
Reinforced binding

Library of Congress Control Number: 2010936722
ISBN: 978 0 975679 1 7

Distributed by Think-a-lot Toys Inc.
www.think-a-lot.com
"Toys and games that make you think"

CPSIA Compliance Information: Batch #1110.
For further information contact
RJ Communications, NY, NY, 1-800-621-2556

Dedicated to all the
fabulous adventures
in your imagination

Now Fabulous Franko,
    who is a friend of mine
Was always very fast
    and the first one off the line

His car was cherry red,
    its tyres shiny black
And when he went out driving,
    he wore a funny hat
He loved to
            go 'round corners

    very VERY
            fast
And only in his nightmares
    was he ever
            EVER last

Until a dreadful day
when fate
would turn a trick
And
Franko drove his little car

onto a
pointy
stick

The tyre lost its air
and the car spun
'round and 'round
And Franko
woke up crying,
his body
on
the
ground

The
car was
scratched and
broken
and
sitting in the mud
And when Franko
sat up smartly,
he fell down with a
thud

His
very best
possession,
his fancy
little car
Not on the road
as normal,
but sitting off the
tar
What would he do,
how could he live
without his love and joy?
"I know" he said "I'm going to
have to find another special toy"
He cried and cried in anger,
"It won't ever be the same"
"I know" he said and smiled
"I'll go and make a plane"

Now Fabulous Franko,
   who is a friend of mine
Only flew his aeroplane
   when the day was nice and fine
He started down the runway
   and pushed the levers high
And as it went into the air,
   his plane began to fly

Round and 'round he flew
and up and down of course
Screaming with delight,
until his voice was hoarse

His fancy little aeroplane
was red in colour too
And you could clearly see him
against the sky so blue

Then one day
   as Franko was flying up so high
Some ugly looking clouds developed in the sky
The air got cold and windy
   and then there came some rain
And suddenly our Franko
   could not control his plane

He pushed the levers this way
   and he pushed the levers that

But then the plane stopped quickly,
   and landed with a Splat!

"Oh no"
he cried

"my plane,
my favourite
love and joy"
"I'm going to have to go
and find another special toy"
He cried and cried in anger
as he put on his best coat

"I suppose I'm going to have to go
and make myself
a boat"

Now Fabulous Franko,
   who is a friend of mine
Loved his little power boat
   and its fancy fishing line

            He took it out to sea
               and rode it on the waves
And if he really wanted to,
   he could stay on it for days
It had a little kitchen, a lounge and bedroom too
In fact it was so fancy, it even had a loo

He could motor on for hours, awash with salty air
And then pull up and anchor,
      to contemplate and stare

He would often
dream of pirates
and all their
daring tales
And
think of
all the
seamen

fighting
vicious gales

He loved the peace and quiet
and fishing on his own
And often called his little boat
      his home away from home

Now, what a
day
our Franko had
with **sun**
and fish
and
beach
Until he drove
his fancy boat
onto a
coral reef

"Oh Blast" he cried "Oh Blimey
my favourite love and joy
I'm going to have to go and find another special toy"
A rocket ship, a motorbike, or perhaps an army tank
"I suppose
I'm going to have
to count my
money in the
bank"

Now Fabulous Franko
    who is a friend of mine
Thought very long and hard
    before going out to buy
He walked into the shop
    and with the money in his pocket
He looked around to see
    he had enough to build a rocket
The rocket took off quickly
    and roared off to the moon
And from its little window
    he could see its long smoke plume

He went 'round all the planets,
      he went 'round all the stars
And then my best friend Franko
      went to visit Mars
Now Franko was quite anxious
      and keen to come back home
So he never left the rocket,
      just peeked out of its dome
He saw some scary Martians
      coming out to play
And that's when clever Franko
      decided NOT to stay

He started up the engines
and roared off with a blast
And came back 'round the planets
super, fiery fast
On coming down to home,
he landed with a crash
His shiny little rocket became a
tangled mash

"Oh no"
he cried another time
"My favourite love and joy
I'm going to have to
go and make
another special toy"

Now Fabulous Franko,
who is a friend of mine
Decided that an army tank
would suit him mighty fine
He drove it through a creek,
and up a big steep hill
And when he slammed
the brakes down fast
The tank stopped
very still
The shiny

BIG red tank
drove on a
funny tread
And made a

BIG fat mess
of his mother's
garden bed

He wore a special suit.
with special
       vision glasses
So he could see at night
and through
   the foggy
      passes

He took it on the sand
and up and down the beach
And to the strangest places,
quite out of normal reach

The army tank was
freedom
and untold joy
and fun

So he could chase
the **baddies**
And get them
on the run

"Oh, Blast! Oh Blimey!"

Until one day our Franko thought up a crazy game
And crashed his army tank whilst driving in the rain

"Oh not again" he cried
"my favourite love and joy"
"Why can't I find an everlasting.
strong and
sturdy toy?"

Now can YOU guess what Franko,
who is a friend of mine
Found for his special toy
on THIS his final time?
He'd smashed his fancy car,
a rocket, plane and tank
And now our poor young Franko
had no money in the bank
What would he do? what could he do
with no money for a toy?
He'd have to think of something else
to give him love and joy

He could
learn to
ski, or skate

or paddle a canoe
And
when you really think of it,
there's a million things to do

To read or cook or play a game
or simply take a walk
To draw a special picture
on a board with nice
white chalk

So next time when you're bored
and can't think of a new game
Just think of our sweet Franko
and you can be the same
Sit still and close your eyes
and concentrate most hard
Then draw the grand ideas
your mind sees on a card

Now this is how we dream
and make our future plans
To always use our minds
and make things
with our
hands

To love and laugh and smile

and have
the best
of friends

To always do our very best
and be happy .....

The END

Franko's
word list
of
differences
between...
British English & American English

tyre ~ tire	motorbike ~ motorcycle
tar ~ pavement or road	loo ~ bathroom
aeroplane ~ airplane	oh blast oh blimey! ~ yikes!
colour ~ color	shop ~ store
favourite ~ favorite	keen to ~ happy to
power boat ~ motor boat	whilst ~ while

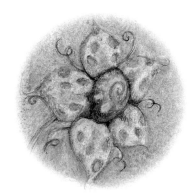